Inhale

A Short Story Collection

Bonnie Ferrante

Inhale: A Short Story Collection

ISBN 978-0-9921037-5-0

Other Books by Bonnie Ferrante

Nightfall - Dawn's End Book 1 (new adult novel)

Poisoned - Dawn's End Book 2 (new adult novel)

Outworld Apocalypse - Dawn's End Book 3 (new adult novel)

Bouquet (short stories)

Terror at White Otter Castle (novella)

Desiccate

Bonnie Ferrante also writes picture books for children.

Table of Contents

"Inhale, and God Approaches You."

~Krishnamacharya

It was Maya's first day at the cottage since the accident. The bicycle leaned against the shed door, front wheel turned backwards. The knots in her chest that made it difficult to breathe, twisted. Maya never wanted to see it again. She had asked her neighbour to take the bike.

Last spring, her nine year old son, Akshay, frustrated that they couldn't bring his BMX on the first trip, had ridden the too-large bicycle. Maya had been unpacking when her only child struck his bare head and died.

Akshay's rooms here and at home were unchanged. Maya had gone into his bedroom once. The sight of his baseball trophy had reduced her to dry, shuddering sobs, gasping for air, collapsed on the floor.

After unpacking, Maya poured a cold drink of water, and went out on the deck. A typed letter was tucked under a decorative stone on an Adirondack chair. The bicycle was gone.

The note explained that it would be given to Bicycles for Humanity. This charity would send it to Africa for those in need of transportation. Medical aid workers were then able to reach people suffering from AIDS. Women who lived too far from the market place were empowered by the ability to sell their wares. Children who lived too far from school could now attend.

Maya envisioned a hot, dusty savannah. She saw the hopeful faces of an AIDS infected family as a nurse arrived on bicycle. She saw the smile on a mother's face as she returned from a successful sale.

Akshay was a child who gave his allowance to Toys for Tots and raised money in the MS Readathon. Maya knew he would be happy the old bicycle was making a difference. She thought of Akshay's BMX gathering dust in the garage at home. Perhaps she could also donate her son's bike. She imagined the joy of a child now able to learn and experience new possibilities for his future. One of the knots in her chest untied.

She carried the letter to the kitchen and left it for her husband. Akshay's yellow raincoat still hung on a peg by the door above his black rubber boots. Some child somewhere could use those to keep dry and warm on a miserable day. She remembered Akshay's warm winter parka and the boy she had seen walking through blowing snow, clutching his thin jacket, the zipper probably broken. She thought of Akshay's ice skates and helmet, his baseball and bat, and all the other sports equipment, clothing, and toys that could make other children's lives a little better.

She could use the grocery boxes to pack what was here. Somewhere a mother was aching because she could not give her child what he wanted or needed. She would take her time to find exactly the right recipients. Maya gave a small smile and took a slow, full breath.

THE END

Sweet William

It is covered with a lavender flock, as pretentious as cheap parlour wallpaper. Arnold's broad shoulders are squeezed into the narrow space, like an overgrown child hiding in a cupboard. A long, white rose lies beside him. Arnold would have preferred a bit of colour. Mary Preston -- no, not Preston anymore -- chose the too-small coffin and the flowers.

There is nothing childlike in Arnold's lined face. Nothing left of my twelve-year-old younger brother who made the trip to Halifax such a long time ago.

* * * * *

Those three days with Aunt Bessie dragged and jerked like cement-dulled skates. She had the voice of a fox-frightened hen and I never knew when she'd descend on me. "Thomas, there's no need to snap off half the bean when you clean it. Thomas, why didn't you empty the slop bucket 'fore it got too heavy to lift? Thomas, the wood's low again." Peck, peck, pecking.

We both rushed to the door when we heard the wagon approach. I knew the news was good the moment I saw their faces.

"Arnold's not retarded," Mother announced even before she had her coat off.

"Well, we all knew *that*," confirmed my aunt as she prepared the tea.

Aunt Bessie had continually said Mother was fooling herself thinking Arnold was anything but brain fried, but no one pointed that out now.

"So, what's the problem?"

"It was the scarlet fever," explained Mother, as she fixed the hair pins in her auburn bun. "His mind's just fine."

"He's deaf," announced Father.

"Deaf?" said Aunt Bessie. "He hears me call him to supper."

"He is too," said Mother. "Not completely, but enough so's he doesn't understand most of what's said. He knows when it's meantime, and if you're calling in his direction, what else could it mean?"

Everyone studied Arnold, who looked from face to face.

"Why's he talk so peculiar?" asked Aunt Bessie.

"Partly because he hasn't heard proper speech since he was three, but mostly because his vocal chords are damaged. Even if he remembered how to say a word from when he was little, it wouldn't come out that way, and he wouldn't know because he can't hear it right."

"Well, Lord love a duck!" announced Aunt Bessie as she crossed her bulging arms.

"If that isn't enough," said Mother, "he probably has bad eyes too."

"So what's to be done?"

"We're going to get him a hearing aid and glasses if he needs them," said Father. "Can't do a thing about the vocal chords. But his speech will improve enough for people to understand."

Everyone stared at Arnold, the eighth wonder of the world. I punched his arm so he'd know I was happy.

"The doctor said there's absolutely nothing wrong with this boy's mind," said Mother. "He may be a bit slower than some, but only because he probably hasn't heard eighty percent of what his parents and teachers have been saying for the last nine years. Imagine that! It's a miracle he's gotten on as well as he has."

Mother burst into tears. Arnold looked bewildered as everyone hugged him and each other in turn.

That Sunday we didn't mind being quiet and spending our time praying, praising the Lord. Mother made sure we were up before the rooster on the Holy Day. Had to meet the Lord shining and clean and ready to receive His word. We all trooped down to St. Michael's Presbyterian and, throughout the service, Reverend Fraser seemed to be thanking the Lord just for us.

* * * * *

Our neighbours, the Prestons, were Roman Catholic. But George Preston only attended services at Christmas and Easter. The rest of the family attended in fits and starts--or whenever the children needed clothes from the church poor box. Mary was our age, and sometimes her dresses hung right to the ground. Our school buddies called her "Mother Mary" and "Mother Hubbard." Arnold didn't know what they were saying. Just as well.

Mary had always snubbed us, especially Arnold who she felt provided a reason to snub a MacDougal. Our farm was twice the size of Preston's and her father George wasn't too successful. Rumour had it he kept a stash of whiskey in the barn. He had seven children and two others in the Catholic Cemetery.

Arnold used to hunch over the plants by the pump, clipping flowers for Mary Preston, his long calloused fingers ignoring the thorns. Even standing, his lanky body hunched, as if he was sinking into his own chest. The neighbours had to admit, though, he had a talent for growing things.

The boys at school weren't impressed; they still called him dummy. After the scarlet fever, Arnold probably hadn't heard what they were saying. If he spoke, they laughed and mocked his speech. He blinked his big grey-blue eyes and turned away. Irene knuckled her little hands on her skinny hips and told them to leave off.

Irene's been my lady for as long as I can remember. I told her once when she took a fancy to the minister's son to give it up, I'd keep after her 'til the last dog was hung. She laughed and said, "No doubt, Thomas." But she didn't laugh when the boys bullied Arnold.

Mary Preston just giggled and dug at the dirt with her shoe. She was a tall, broad girl, with stringy brown hair, a long nose and pale blue eyes. O' course, that's not how Arnold saw her.

It was the school teacher, Sarah West, who talked Mother into taking Arnold to Halifax. Mother's voice was insistent when she talked to Father. So unlike her. I listened through the stove pipe hole from my bedroom above the kitchen.

"Miss West says he understands very quickly when people show him what to do. She thinks there's something else wrong. That he's not . . . "

"Retarded?" finished Father.

Father was always one for facing facts. "Admit your mistakes and take your punishment," he'd say in his deep soft voice. His face was large and tanned, white lined where the crow's feet danced around his eyes. He was tall and broad-shouldered with large, strong hands.

"I know it's hard," Father continued. "He was such a bright little one. But that scarlet fever overheated his brain. He'll never be normal."

"He is normal," countered Mother. "He doesn't have to be like everyone else to be normal. I want him to be happy. He's clever with his hands and good with the animals. Once he caught on to numbers he learned his sums and table real quick. I think Doctor Kimlock was wrong. I want to take him to Halifax." She paused a moment and said, "He's twelve, Jack. We've got to find out for sure before he's all growed up and it's too late."

At last, Father gave in. They'd visit Aunt Bessie the following day. If she could take care of me, Bert could handle the farm.

* * * * *

The day Arnold got his hearing aid everyone talked in such loud, excited voices he probably could have heard us without it. It was a bit smaller than those little Walkmans they have today and sat in his chest pocket with a thin cord running to the plug in his ear. For weeks, Arnold walked around looking astonished at every sound. The thing whistled and crackled with any quick movement, but Arnold couldn't stop smiling. I figured it wouldn't be long before he'd be talking up a storm, but he became even quieter.

"I talk stupid," he told me once.

I guess he never knew how he sounded.

"So what?" I said. "Say intelligent things and no one will take notice."

He must have heeded my advice. He moved to the front row at school and soaked up every word Miss West spoke. But his ears still flamed when she called on him. Even when he had the answer, he stood staring at his feet until she let him sit back down.

One chilly afternoon, Miss West asked Ed Irvine a question about King George. Irvine was a fat bully with scaly skin and no eyelashes, who take pleasure tormenting the little ones. Ed picked at his warty hands.

"Stand up Edward," ordered Miss West. She repeated the question.

Before Ed could mumble something, Arnold shouted out the answer. There was a surprised silence, then the students burst into laughter. Arnold looked around. I smiled at him so he'd know they weren't laughing at him. "Yes, Arnold, that's right," said Miss West. She smiled and ignored that he'd failed to raise his hand. "You're certainly enthusiastic about the royal family."

Ed glared as he sat down.

I was away the next day. Just a little cough, but Mother insisted on smothering me in a mustard and garlic plaster and keeping me in bed. While I was going up in flames, Ed and his buddies cornered Arnold by the well. Tommy Turner, who didn't join in but was too cowardly to stand up to Ed, told me about it.

"Turning into a smart mouth, eh, MacDougal?" Ed sneered.

Arnold shook his head no.

"What's the matter? Can't talk? Or maybe this ain't turned up enough." He poked the hearing aid with his finger. The box crackled and whined in a high pitch. Arnold jerked the plug out of his ear. The boys laughed and taunted him.

I don't know how they made him do it, especially since he was feeling good about school. But, that afternoon, Arnold climbed into the crawl space under the roof. The trap door was near the teacher's desk and was always left partly open. When Miss West passed underneath, he dumped a box of crushed chalk and chalk dust on her.

There was no chance Miss West would favour Arnold again. He was so ashamed, he didn't say a word when Father took him to the woodshed.

A couple of weeks later, Arnold received his first pair of glasses. We made a day of the trip into Dartmouth, leaving right after chores. Arnold sat in stunned silence for the return trip, his mouth and eyes big open circles.

After supper, he stood by the front window. I joined him and we stared down the lane. "I never knew you could see the mailbox from the house," he whispered. I swallowed hard and asked him what he could see before.

"A blur of trees and dirt. Now I can even see the clouds."

Arnold was looked upon with some envy by the other students. Mary Preston stared wistfully. Not many parents would spend that much money on a hearing aid and glasses for their young one. Our family's esteem rose.

Arnold still talked oddly and had gaps in understanding but he was always smiling and polite. Few took pleasure in calling him dummy anymore. He tore right through the senior second reader. Even the nickname "four eyes" faded.

On the last day of school before summer holidays, When Arnold was fourteen, he stopped to gather purple irises from the garden. He stood them in a McCormick's Assorted Candies tin.

"Who's that for?" I asked as we walked to school. "Got a girl?"

Arnold blushed, but he didn't answer. He left them anonymously on Miss West's desk. "Oh, I love flowers," gushed Mary Preston, as all the girls crowded around to smell them.

Arnold smiled and fingered his shirt cuff. I'd noticed him staring at Mary when he thought she wasn't watching.

Off and on that summer, I saw Arnold arranging blue and red sweet William in a peanut brittle can. They weren't for Mother, and I thought it was strange that he would bring Miss West flowers now. Maybe he still felt guilty about dumping the chalk.

One evening, I followed him down the west lane out to the Preston farm where he left the flowers on the splintery back steps.

The next summer, Arnold continued to deliver flowers: yellow chrysanthemums, pale blue carnations, lavender, and fire-engine red roses. Once he came racing back up the lane, as if the bull had got loose.

"What's the matter?" I teased. "Mary see you?"

She had, of course, and he looked stunned. Both of us confronting his secret in the same day was just too much.

"So, what did she say?" I pressed.

"Nothing."

Neither of us mentioned the flowers come September. When Mary saw him watching her, she would smile quickly, then turn away. Arnold would get this hopeless, confused expression. It was his last year at school. He was doing an adult's work on the farm.

The following summer, a week before Commonwealth Day, I saw him cutting deep pink hybrid tea roses.

"Why don't you just give them to her, instead of leaving them on the doorstep. She won't eat you."

Arnold flinched, then shrugged.

"Go on. Just knock on the door."

"Can't do that," he muttered. "Too many kids.

"Wait outside for her. She's got to come out to do her chores. Give them to her then. What's the point of bringing her flowers if you never talk to her?"

"What do I say?"

"Just talk to her like you talk to me. It isn't so hard once you get started. I talk to Irene about all sorts of things."

Returning, Arnold strode into the yard as if he'd just completed a cross country march. There was a big sweat mark on the back of his shirt, although it wasn't a hot day.

"Well?" I demanded.

"I asked her if she was going to the box social?"

"Is she?"

Arnold nodded. "I asked her to put a rose on her lunch box so's I'd know it was hers and I could bid on it." His eyes looked like blue ponds through the thick glasses. His shifted his feet and his hearing aid whistled. "I'm going to eat lunch with her," he whispered.

At the appointed day, Mary wrapped her lunch box in pink tissue paper and put a pink rose on top. I saw her carrying it in. The flower was wilting.

Women's Auxiliary tables covered the sawhorses and sheets of wood. There were fancy embroidered linens, orderly cross-stitched ginghams, and crocheted pineapples. We laughed and elbowed one another, circling the riches, guessing which box belonged to which girl and the possible contents -- juicy fried chicken, spicy cooked ham, cool cucumber sandwiches. I made a big show of being interested in this box or that one.

"Aren't you going to buy Irene's?" Arnold whispered.

"Of course. I'm just having a bit of fun with her."

"Irene's a nice girl," Arnold said.

I laughed. "I know. She made potato salad and smoked salmon slices. I wouldn't pass that up now, would I? You know which one you're bidding on?"

"The pink one with the rose," said Arnold with his shy smile.

"What if it belongs to Ed's ugly sister?"

"Oh, no. It belongs to the prettiest girl here."

I laughed again. "Then it may cost more than you can afford."

Paul Smith and Murray McDonald decided to challenge my bid. Irene wouldn't have given them the time of day. There was also a new man bidding, name of Jack

Seagrum. He sold combines and was spending the holiday with his sister and her family. I wondered how a young girl might feel having to eat her lunch with him. They watched while he bid. He had a moustache like Errol Flynn and wore fine clothes. He bid on almost every box that was auctioned. It seemed as though he was helping to raise the price and not interested in winning. Then a pink tissue-wrapped box was held up.

"Isn't that the one you wanted?" I asked Arnold.

"No. There's no rose."

When the bidding closed, Jack leapt onto the platform to claim his prize.

"And whose the lovely lady that made this lunch?" called the auctioneer.

Mary Preston stepped forward. She smiled at Jack, who bowed graciously in return. Arnold turned pale, and his face sagged, as if someone had punched the air out of him.

A few days later, Mary told Arnold to stop brining her flowers. Jack Seagrum was seen at the Preston farm every night.

In the weeks that followed, Arnold let the weeds twine their pervasive way through the rose bushes. I couldn't bear to see them choking, so I cleared them one morning after milking.

"You weed the roses?" Arnold asked at supper.

I admitted to it.

"No need," he said.

"They shouldn't be left to die. Plenty of girls like roses."

Arnold's head jerked up. He met my look, then shook his head slowly. "Give them to Irene," he muttered.

* * * * *

Mary left town with Jack Seagrum. Some say Old George threw her out because she was in the family way. Arnold took up tending the roses again. He gave some to Mother and some to Irene, but most ended up in the compost. He planted few annuals.

We lost track of Mary Preston. Mother passed on during the bitter winter of '49. Father died under the hay wagon a year later. I married Irene and brought her to live on the farm. She tried to matchmake Arnold with several women, but gave up when he barely spoke.

On our seventh anniversary, Arnold took care of the two young ones so we could drive to Dartmouth. We went for a restaurant meal and caught the motion picture *A Streetcar Named Desire.*

When we arrived home late that night, Irene made tea for the three of us. The two newest MacDougals were asleep upstairs.

"You'll never guess who we saw in town," cried Irene as she sipped her tea.

My kick missed her and hit the table leg.

"Mary Preston. Remember her?"

Arnold's cup dropped to the saucer with a clink. His tea splashed.

"Seems the wonderful Jack Seagrum's run out on her and three little ones."

"Th-three!" stuttered Arnold.

"I'm pretty sure they never did marry either. Those poor kids. What a burden, being, you know . . . . My children are so fortunate to have a father like Thomas."

I had to forgive her.

"How Mary's going to support them alone on a second cook's pay and no one to help--"

"'Cuse me," muttered Arnold. He stood, dumped his tea into the slop bucket and went upstairs.

At breakfast, he announced that he was going to Dartmouth.

I gave him my best look of discouragement while Irene showed great interest in her tea. He looked steadily back at me.

"For how long?" I asked.

"A week, maybe more. I'll stop by Ferguson's and hire his boy to help while I'm gone."

"No need. We can manage for a week."

"Might be more, Thomas. I'll pay him."

What could I say to a grown man who'd been alone while I was raising a family?

They were married soon after. Irene and I were witnesses. Mary carried a bouquet of roses, baby's breath, and sweet William from our garden.

Arnold saw a lawyer and changed the children's names to MacDougal. I didn't like the idea much, but it wasn't just my name. He brought them to live on the farm. Suddenly the house was filled with shrill voices.

Irene coped with the crowding as best she could, bless her heart. She tried to make it seem like their home as well.

Arnold built an extension off the back and divided it into two rooms. Mary's children worshipped him, particularly little Bobby who followed him around like a newly hatched duckling.

All summer long there were flowers in a Blue Ribbon coffee can on the kitchen table. It hurt me to have to show Arnold the empty vodka bottle.

"It's just one bottle," he said.

"It's the third one I've found. Mary's been odd lately."

"The women have been giving her a rough time. They snub her at church. Say she doesn't belong there."

"I see."

"It's none of their damn business. She's my wife. She's got nothing to be ashamed of."

I told him the night before last I'd found her asleep at the kitchen table. "Bobby was outside alone after dark."

"I'll take care of Bobby. It's none of your damn business either."

He glared at me, his eyes as sharp as sickles. I shouldn't have interfered between a man and his wife.

The next day at supper, Mary left the kitchen twice. Each time she returned, she seemed more irritated. When Bobby spilled a glass of milk, she slapped him.

"I'll get it," said Arnold.

"I'll get it," mimicked Mary, copying his stumbly speech

The kitchen clock ticked in the silence. The children looked at their plates. Bobby sniffed.

The families started eating meals separately. Irene and I let them eat first, but that had its drawbacks. Arnold would join Mary for a few drinks afterward and their voices would get louder and louder.

"Why don't you answer me?" we heard Mary say one night. "I know why. 'Cos you got nothing to say. Nothing from nothing."

Arnold's voice was a low rumble.

Irene told me it upset her stomach listening to them while she ate. Her pregnancy was a good excuse to switch. She said she was too hungry to wait, so she and I and our two young ones began eating first.

It wasn't much better. Sometimes they started drinking before supper.

"What's the matter with you? Turn that damn thing up if you can't hear me?" Mary yelled.

"I hear you."

"I hear you! I hear you! Then why don't you ever understand me?"

I could see Arnold from where I sat. He sighed and turned down the volume on his hearing aid. It whistled shrilly, and Mary leapt to her feet. She ran into the kitchen and began smashing plates on the floor, one after another, in a steady rhythm. Irene jumped up but I grabbed her arm. They were Mary's dishes.

A few days later, Mary let a soup pot boil dry on the stove. Irene was frightened. The next morning the house still smelled of smoke.

The following week they left. There were farming jobs in Manitoba.

* * * * *

The next Christmas I received a card with a note inside. I read it to Irene.

"I broke my leg last month and been bedridden. Mary's working as a cook. Doing all right but it'll be a bare Christmas. Hope you're doing well. God bless. Love, Arnold."

We looked at each other, and I said, "I'll send him what I can."

I never expected to be heading west myself. But soon after, our littlest one developed asthma. After a few close calls, the doctor advised that we move off the farm to a drier climate -- the Maritimes were too wet and cold.

I got a job in a grain elevator in Port Arthur, Ontario. I used to think that some of the wheat coming through might have been cut by Arnold.

I never was much good at letter writing. Arnold neither. We exchanged cards at Christmas, but they didn't really say much. We went to visit once. Mary's hair was mostly grey and her clothes were stained with grease spots. Arnold was quieter than ever, and he stooped like an old man. The prairie wind never stopped blowing.

* * * * *

I'm surprised they left Arnold's coffin open. I thought he'd be smashed up. Mr. Rantz, the mortician, did a good job.

Four men came out to the funeral from the first farm he worked on, and others from other places. I could tell they respected him. He always was a hard worker -- fair and honest. More than one said they could count on him. The lad who drove the combine didn't come. Must have been a hard lesson.

I thought Mary'd be hysterical, or maybe falling down drunk, but she preened under all the attention. Kept telling everyone how Arnold used to bring her sweet William from his garden when they were still in school and how he always managed to get her flowers on her birthday, even between jobs.

Bobby, her oldest, has all grown up into a shaggy-haired young man. He seldom speaks. Reminds me of

Arnold in a way. But Arnold wouldn't have approved of the glares he gives his mother. He said he could tell I was Arnold's brother, we look alike.

The cemetery is one of those modern places with flat headstones you can mow over. No one's allowed to plant flowers on the graves. I'd brought some sweet William seeds, though I doubt they'd survive in the dry wind anyway. Arnold's the first in four generations not to be buried down home.

When Mary and the others had said their goodbyes to Arnold, I stepped forward and said to Mr. Rantz, "One moment please, I'd like to take this white rose."

"Would you like me to remove his glasses?" whispered Mr. Rantz.

I looked at Arnold and thought of the day he'd brought his first pair of glasses home -- how he'd gone to the front window, able at last to see clearly what the world had to offer.

"Leave them where they are," I said, and I stepped back, turning the rose in my hands.

THE END

The Colour of...

(Flash Fiction)

The building was spray painted "dykes are damned!" the colour of a matador's cape. Letters dribbled in blood-like streams. The words hadn't registered until today.

I picked my way through the alley avoiding coffee cups, candy wrappers, and a condom. A ribbon was on the grey sidewalk outside the bar, a splash of Christmas colour. The colour of joy.

Inside, everyone talked about the fire. My friends hadn't arrived, so I sat at the bar, ordered a beer and listened.

"Nobody *has* to risk their life for another person," said a girl with strawberry hair and lipstick. She enunciated each word as if diction equalled truth.

"What about that bystander law? Don't they have to at least call the cops?" asked a skinny guy. He kept touching an infected piercing on his lip, the colour of a fever.

"For sure!" said another guy. This one was muscled, black t-shirt, and had ultra short black hair with a cherry streak, the colour of passion. "Christ, how much trouble is a phone call?"

"I'm not saying they shouldn't have phoned," replied the girl. "I'm just saying you don't have to throw yourself on the person or something and risk getting burned. Or try to fight off a gang of crazies."

My beer arrived and I took a long drink.

"Maybe they were afraid the gang might turn on them," suggested the skinny guy.

"For a phone call?" said Muscles. "They could'a just walked around the corner and no one would know. I heard they stood there watching."

"How does anyone know that," asked the girl, "unless they were there too?"

Skinny shrugged. "It was on Facebook. I heard there's a video circulating. One of the bystanders put it on video. The cops got it."

"That's just sick," said the girl. "I hope his family never sees it."

"All he did was volunteer at the AIDS center," said Skinny. "I don't think he was even gay."

"Like the fuck that matters," said Muscles.

I nodded to myself. I'd heard the jokes about flaming gays.

The day it happened, I was on a coffee break. I put chocolate sprinkles in my coffee and Sam said, "That's just gay." We laughed.

Skinny changed the subject. I finished off my drink and decided to wait outside. The room felt hot and stuffy.

The ribbon was still there. Unclaimed. Ignored. Slowly blending in with all the other trash. It was the colour of violence and blood. The colour of war. I thought about how many times I'd looked away.

I picked up the ribbon with a pin still attached. It was the colour of a target. A vivid crimson ribbon.

The colour of apples, hearts and love.

The colour of strength.

The colour of a stop sign.

I wiped it on my jeans and pinned it on. I have some grey spray paint I can use. It should cover up that graffiti pretty well. And, well, maybe they could use some help at the AIDS center.

THE END

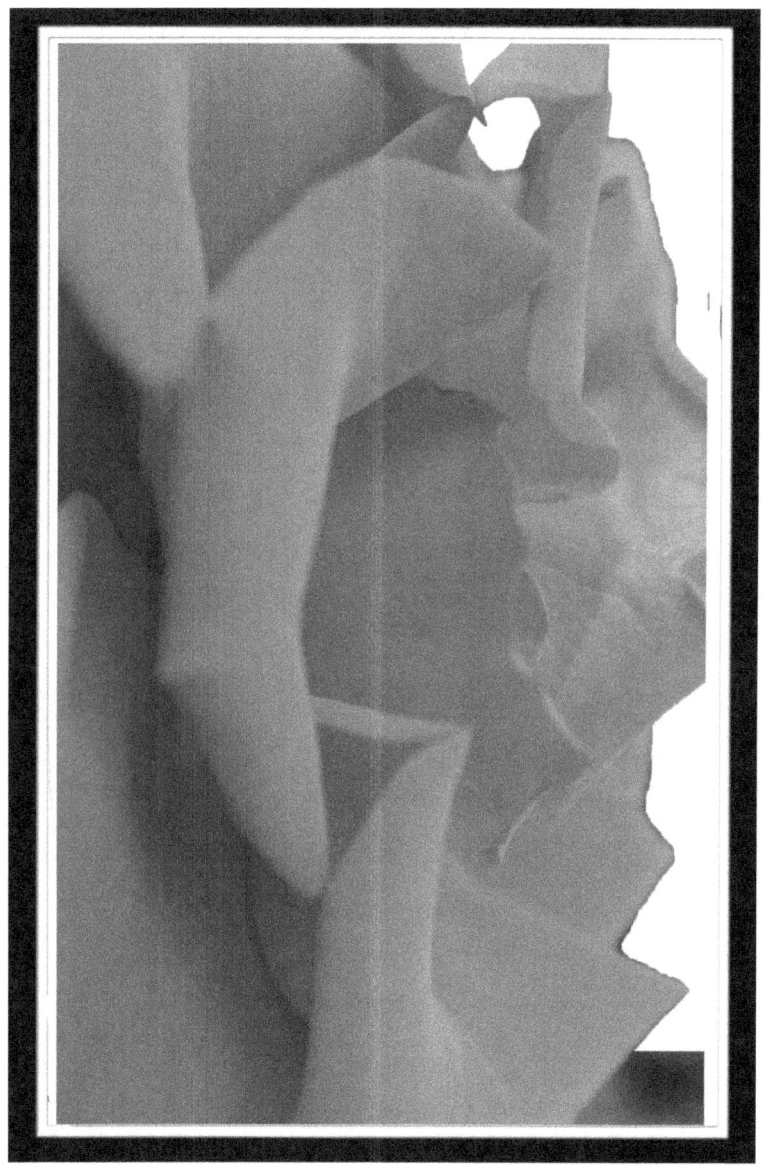

Aberrations

Maureen covered her ears, trying to mute the grind of machines, the shrieking of passengers, and the drone of hawkers "Black and White" and "American Pie" boomed from loudspeakers Her teeth stung from a candy apple and her neck was twisted from The Mad Mouse. No wonder Tom had vomited. The smell of dirt mingled with burgers and corn and livestock, like filthy hands pressing against her face.

Tom was embarrassed. Soldiers did not get ill from carnival rides. Coming to the CLE had been his idea. It was something they had done together before they'd married, before he'd lost his job and signed up to serve his country.

Maureen was reluctant. The signs advertising snake men, two-headed cows, and bearded ladies made her skin crawl. But it was impossible to argue with Tom's toothy grin and teddy bear brown eyes. She'd put him through enough lately. She'd try to make the next two days pleasant.

"Will you be all right?" he asked, clutching his stomach.

"Of course. Go to the washroom until you feel better," said Maureen. "I'll meet you at the Milk Bottle. I'll buy you a tea."

Tom rolled up his sleeves. She looked away, not wanting to see the scar he'd gotten on his last tour. The reminder that in two days, he would be back harm's way, all her stability disappearing over the horizon.

Families swirled past. Mothers pushing babies in strollers. Wan faced toddlers on their fathers' backs. Giggling girls dragging their worn out parents. She didn't want to tell Tom. There would be no more sedatives, or trips to the O.H., the hospital for loonies and wives who attempt suicide.

She watched him thread through the crowd. He bounced on the balls of his feet when he walked. It made him look taller than he really was. Had he walked like that as a toddler, springing across the floor in his baby shoes? Would their baby have walked like that? If it had grown legs?

She juggled all the expectations, circling the coloured balls of normality in a careful balance. She mustn't let them fall again, even when they changed into burning torches. That would "cause concern."

She forced herself to stop, to lower her hands. Since she left the hospital, she'd kept away from daydreams of what she would never have. Nightmares of what she did have on the bathroom floor. The doctor had said being knocked to the ground by the purse-snatcher may have triggered the miscarriage. Maureen knew it wasn't his hands that had caused it, but his cold fierce eyes.

Tom said they could adopt, but the waiting period was years. Did mothers give away babies with teddy bear brown eyes and bouncy walks? She commanded her thoughts to stop, her legs to move.

Maureen headed toward the food stands, but paused in front of a red and yellow billboard, painted with a childish scrawl. FIERCE RARE CREATURES FROM THE JUNGLES OF AFRICA AND TROPICAL FORESTS OF INDIA. She heard an adolescent boy as he emerged complaining that the display was just dumb monkeys. A smile twitched at the corners of her mouth.

She remembered the pictures of Diane Fossey and the gorillas, Jane Goodall and the chimpanzees, that she and her father would pour over in National Geographic. They loved the way the troop members groomed each other, picking off the nits, laying on the grass with total abandon. Her eyes had widened at the photograph of bluffing, until her father explained that the displaying primate tore up the vegetation to establish dominance. They were usually gentle creatures, supportive of each other, and protective of their young. An entire troop was often butchered to capture one black market baby.

Maureen was shocked that poachers would trap a gorilla in a wire snare, and then amputate his head and hands. "Hands," her father said, "some pervert would use as an ashtray."

Three years ago, just two weeks after her wedding, her father had telephoned, filled with excitement at the news that Peanuts had touched Diane Fossey's hand, the first physical contact between her and a gorilla.

Not long after, her father had been murdered by a drug addict who didn't realize his victim was dead long before he stopped stabbing. Maureen had found him half a block from home.

Maureen still had the stuffed toy gorilla he'd given her on the desk in her bedroom. She only had to hug it to relive the sensation of sitting in the huge armchair, perusing the glossy magazine pages, her father's deep voice in her ear, the smell of his Old Spice Aftershave enveloping her.

* * * * *

The ticket collector caught her eye. He was a dwarf with crooked nose and black teeth. He stared at her, challenging her not to look away. A cigarette dangled from the corner of his mouth.

"Cost two tickets, pretty lady," he called in his high voice. "See exotic creatures from around the world."

Without thought, she dug out the price. His hands were dirty and there was a nasty scar above one wrist, like a bite mark.

The trailer had an exit and an entrance, one on each end. Maureen's runners clanged on the stairs. She expected it to open up into a large tent, but instead there was a single long, rectangular box inside, like a metal storage tank at a fish hatchery. At the other end, near the second exit, bails of hay were piled. She looked into the steel box through the wire grid top. It was divided into two sections. She could see into the first half. The metal floor had a scattering of straw. It stank.

There was a small bundle of fur, beige with dark brown tips, curled tightly in one corner. The sign above the cage read MACACA RHESUS. The monkey adjusted its position, clawed outwards, pulling the dirty straw under its body. The tiny hands were covered with pure white hair like the down on a newborn baby.

The monkey turned around. It was male, and too young to be taken from his mother. He scratched his shoulder, stretching, trying to reach the middle of his back. There was no one to groom his fur. His large brown eyes were empty. He sighed and curled tightly back into a ball. Maureen tasted hay and dung in the back of her throat.

She didn't want to look in the second cage. She glanced at the sign in passing. CONGO PAN PANISCUS. The rattle of a chain drew her attention. Her feet stopped moving. She didn't want to look, but she did. Down into the metal cage, through the grid of wire, at the shackled body of a chimpanzee. There were manacles on one arm and one leg, attached to a chain which was bolted to the floor. The straw was filthy and the animal reeked. With his free hand, he rubbed straw on the metal cuff around his ankle. He pushed the cuff up, then rubbed, then down and rubbed. The fur around his ankle was gone and the flesh was pink and weeping. A cyst had formed above the cuff. He looked into Maureen's face. His eyes were black and dead.

Suddenly he screamed. Maureen flinched. Frustration, fury, horror. He screamed at her and threw straw. It flew around the metal box and fell back onto his face. He jerked to his feet, the chain clanging, and lunged for Maureen, screaming and screaming. Maureen felt invisible balls strike her face.

The trailer swayed as she pounded down the steps. She ran and pushed. Past the mothers with healthy bodies and their fully formed babies. Past fathers, toddlers, teenagers, all oblivious to the horror in their midst. She shoved through the crowd of people lined up at the entrance. She ran blindly, leaving behind the Mad Mouse, the Double Ferris Wheel, and the Milk Bottle where her husband waited.

* * * * *

Tom had searched the fair grounds for two hours before driving home. He had listened to Maureen's sobbing and did not reply to her incoherent story. Words shot from her mouth like flames. She knew she was frightening him, giving him visions of her with wrists and ankles strapped to the hospital bed, but she couldn't stop.

When she could no longer cry, he rocked her in his arms while she hiccupped. He made cocoa and handed her a sedative, the bottle locked safely away. Maureen slipped the medication inside her pillowcase.

They listened to the radio. Maureen shut if off when Helen Reddy declared "She is Woman." They cuddled in bed together with their steaming mugs. Tom chastised himself for leaving her alone.

"You didn't know," Maureen said.

"How could people do that?" he asked.

Maureen shook her head, cupping the warm cocoa in her hands. She remembered the last time she went to a sideshow. They were travelling through New Orleans, an old and mysterious city. She was a small girl at the time.

She walked with her father, holding his large calloused hand. They saw an enormous poster with the painting of two men joined at the waist.

"Daddy! What's that?"

"Siamese twins."

"Can we see them?"

"They're not here. That's a picture of famous brothers who travelled with Barnum and Bailey for a while. It's probably just a cow with two heads or a couple of sheep stuck together at the rump."

"Can we see them? Please?"

Her father was reluctant, but she persisted. By the time he bought the two tickets and joined the long line, they learned that it was indeed two joined humans.

"Probably just a trick," said her father. "After the fair closes down, these sideshow people take off all their makeup and props and they don't look much different from us."

The exhibit was inside a grand canvas tent. Maureen was amazed at the long line, almost as big as at the huge Ferris Wheel. When they finally made their way inside, the crowd was hushed, speaking in whispers. She took her father's hand and they pushed their way to the front.

There was a glass chamber, the size of a small bedroom. Piled in the centre was a large set of wooden building blocks. Two little boys, wearing sailor suits, sat behind them. They were joined at the back of one shoulder.

One child played with the blocks, while the other stared back at the dozens of spectators peering in. Maureen waved. He looked blankly at her, his hands limp in his lap.

There were only blocks in the room. No rubber balls. No cars and trucks.

"What if one wants to go somewhere and the other one doesn't?" Maureen asked her father.

He pressed his lips tightly together and led her outside. They stood in the sunshine while he took two deep breaths. He removed his glasses and wiped his eyes with his handkerchief.

"How could they do that?" he whispered.

Maureen didn't know who he meant.

* * * * *

The house was dark and silent; sounds of the fair clawed at her windows. She went into the spare bedroom, the one that would now be a hobby room, a place where sewing and painting could substitute for nursing and storytelling. From the high window, she could still locate the lights of the fair in the middle of the city.

The mute house gnawed at her like a parasite. Tom would be sharing a room with strange men, who snored, grunted and talked in their sleep. In spite of all her promises, Maureen had barely eaten since Tom began his tour of duty yesterday. Neither did she call any of their friends. She sat in the rocking chair and listened to the taunt of the carnival until it closed. The dwarf's face challenged her.

At three a.m., she slipped on her jacket and put her flashlight in her empty pocket, a candle and matches as backup. She took the three sedatives from her pillowcase, a banana and the crowbar from the basement.

Few cars passed as she headed to the fairgrounds. She squeezed around the end of the chain link fence along the river.

Spider-like eyes of the silent rides crawled on her back. The trailers were quiet as tombs. The sideshow door was padlocked. She circled it, stepped up on the side and tried to peer in through the ventilation slats. It was dark.

When she forced the lock, the chimpanzee screeched an alarm. Maureen replaced the lock and hid. No one came.

The macaque was still curled in a ball. Maureen didn't dare go near the chimpanzee. Inside, the smell was overpowering, the air tart and gritty. She set the flashlight on the floor; the cage cast a shadow on the ceiling. She opened the banana, broke it in half, embedded two sedatives in one part and the third in the other. She gently lobbed the doubly laced banana into the chimpanzee's cage and dropped the other piece into the macaque's. Maureen sat on the cold floor, her back to the wall and her knees pulled into her chest. When the sounds of eating stopped, she waited a quarter hour for the medication to work.

Her light beam scoured the cage for a door, but Maureen realized the monkeys entered from outside the trailer. She couldn't risk standing in the open. She slid the crowbar under the wire frame and lifted. The monkey sat up and watched. The lid creaked and stretched, but stayed in place. It was beyond her strength.

Maureen would not be able to free him. What would she do with him if even if she did? And the chimpanzee? The macaque whimpered and chewed at his arm. He was beginning to wear away the fur. It was hopeless. They were trapped until death in the freak show, becoming more and more grotesque.

Maureen crept along the trailer. She piled the bales of straw against the other exit. The macaque whimpered again and the chimpanzee shook the wire roof of his cage.

Burning is a painful death. Maureen hoped the smoke would suffocate them before the flames enter their cages, before the straw under them flared. The match flared briefly before she dropped it on the bale at the far end. She walked back to the opposite entrance and pulled the door shut. She would wait to make sure it worked.

Flames crackled softly as the smoke twisted upwards. The chimpanzee screeched. He thumped the cage and screamed and screamed.

A door slammed. Men would put out the fire. The monkeys would never be free. Maureen jammed the door beside her with the crow bar. She must give the fire time to get control.

Men shouted and pounded on the door, one voice a high-pitched demand. The other exit, where the bale of hay burned, was chained from the inside. As long as this door held, they could not get in.

The macaque cried a small child's wail. Maureen went to him. There was a gap along the edge of his cage where she had tried to force it open. She could just squeeze her hand through. The metal carved shallow slits into the skin on her arm.

The macaque stared at Maureen's wiggling hand. Smoke stung her eyes.

"Don't be afraid," she said. "Everything's okay now."

Slowly, he moved towards her. The chimpanzee continued his uproar. The trailer rocked with his frenzied lunges and the pounding of the men. The macaque edged closer.

"It's all right," she told him. She coughed. "Don't be afraid."

He pressed his lips against her fingers like a kiss. She pushed her arm further inside and scratched the top of his overly large head. He arched against her as Maureen caressed his small shoulder. She started to pull her arm out, but the wires dug deeply into her skin, like claws.

Pain tore through her body as she twisted. Maureen screamed. As the blood dripped down Maureen's arm the monkey flinched away. The wire grated against bone.

The chimpanzee's howls became croaks.

Maureen stopped straining. She pressed her cheek against the grid of wire. What was the use? The baby monkey lifted his head slowly and gazed at her with large brown eyes. Teddy bear eyes. She wished she could have struggled more, but she could not bear the waiting, day by day, expecting the news of one more grisly death. The monkey took her thumb in his tiny hand. She smiled. He rubbed his crooked nose on the back of her hand and then bared his blackened teeth.

THE END

Window Dressing

Anita rubbed her brow and turned toward the bed. She stopped, startled. The curtains were open with a clear view into the neighbour's garden. Mr. Cerroni, in his red plaid shirt and green work pants, was pulling weeds in the cooling evening. She watched for a few seconds. Intent on his chores, he probably hadn't noticed her undressing after work.

Poor old guy. Ever since his wife died, all he does is work that damn vegetable patch. He might as well not even have relatives, for all the company they give him. At least, when he is gardening, he's not slugging back the homemade wine.

As she adjusted the curtains, Mr. Cerroni glanced up.

Did he see me move? If he can see me now, he must have seen me with the lights on.

She peeked through the window while the white-haired man continued down his rows.

This is stupid. If he saw me, he saw me. Give the old guy a thrill.

She smoothed her white uniform on the hanger. There were two black smudges on the left hip, but she could wear it another day. *If one more jerk rams me with a cart, I'm make him eat it.* She pried off her shoes, pausing to rub at a scuff.

She propped up her pillows and half lay, half sat on the bed. In her large bedroom, the gleam of mahogany was dulled by a gradual accretion of dust. Bare carpets, scarred by indentations of absent furniture, lay throughout the rest of the three-bedroom bungalow. The kitchen suite was intact, but the dining room empty. The living room held a white wicker rocker, its canes split like barbed wire, and an old shoe box of CDs, useless without the player. The spare room was bare.

Often she felt like this house, a collection of atoms through which cold drafts could flow unhindered by any solid monuments to the past. She had sold her personal things, too—the sewing machine, her Dresden dolls, even her jewellery.

Still, whatever, she wouldn't sell the house. There had been too many late nights alone, painting, wallpapering, laying carpets. Two years left on the mortgage when she had caught him on the couch with the little bitch from the Marina. The couch was the first furniture she had let him take.

She lay there considering the fresh, crunchy vegetables in the garden next door. She imagined the minerals and vitamins surging through her body. In her own small plot, dandelions, crabgrass, thistles, and vetch were on the verge of smothering what was edible, a far cry from her expectations. She felt beaten by their persistence. She glanced at the clock—9:20 p.m. Tomorrow she would tackle the weed-pit. Right now she should make something to eat, but. . . .

She woke with her wrinkled slip twisted under her back. The digital clock read 11:06 p.m. Her stomach growled. She tugged on her slippers, one toe peeking out the end, wrapped her house coat over her slip and shuffled into the kitchen. In the first cupboard she found three cans of soup, in the next four packages of Kraft Dinner and an opened onion soup mix with the tinfoil rolled down. The bang of the cupboard doors echoed through the dining room. In the third cupboard, she found a tin of sardines, a can of spaghetti sauce and a package of Chinese noodles.

She munched on the last apple while eating the macaroni and cheese from the pot. She washed the dishes and brought the mail to the bedroom.

She peeled off her pantyhose, stitched the hole in the toe, and liberally covered it with nail polish. It was her last pair.

There's not enough money for the hydro bill, she thought, *and I can't buy groceries.*

It wasn't as though she'd always had regular mealtimes. Her mother cooked when she thought of it. By the time she was five, Anita knew enough to feed herself when she was hungry, when there was food available.

She remembered helping her mother pack and unpack, evicted from apartment after apartment for delinquent rent. Her mother was always distracted, often unreachable. Twice Anita had stayed in foster homes while her mother pulled her life together. Her foster parents had done a better job of providing food and shelter, but little in the way of nurturing. Her mother had overdosed on prescription drugs when Anita was fifteen.

She would never live like that. This house was hers. She was glad she had no family to hassle her into selling. She could make it on her own.

She fell asleep still hungry and woke ravenous. After a breakfast of Scotch broth, she dressed for the garden attack in her bleach-stained, mauve jogging pants, a frayed white shirt, old winter gloves and rain boots. The grass was heavy with dew.

She yanked a thistle as tall as her knee from the lettuce row and flung it across the lawn. In the short northern growing season, vegetables needed diligent coaxing. The native weeds thrived even on frost and drought. Mr. Cerroni stood by his bean poles, watching her. *The hell with him and his Eden.* She tugged at a clump of chickweed. *Damn his greenhouse.* The plant released dirt in a shower. She threw it across the garden. *As soon as the house is paid for, I plant grass.*

"How's the lettuce?" called Mr. Cerroni over the fence.

Anita jumped at the sudden voice. "Buried," she said.

"You got a difficult life," he said in his heavy Italian accent. "Work all day. Run a house alone."

Anita studied his weather-browned face. He smiled.

"It doesn't give me much time to garden," she said. "I'm lucky if I get the grass cut."

"Well. . . now there's just me at home, I grow more than I eat. My lettuces, she's going to overshoot. You *Take* some."

"Sure!"

The old man disappeared for a few minutes while Anita continued her assault on the intruders.

"Couple of salads," said the neighbour, setting a paper bag on top of the fence.

"Thanks, Mr. Cerroni."

As soon as her neighbour had left, Anita reached into the bag, pulled some lettuce from the top, rinsed it under the hose, and ate it while she worked. When the weeds had been stuffed into a large black garbage bag, she mowed the lawn. It was mid-afternoon before she retrieved the paper bag from the bag fence. It felt too heavy for lettuce, and when she opened it, she discovered young carrots, radishes, parsley, and sweet red strawberries.

Two weeks later, on a Friday, a co-worker treated her to a couple of vodkas after work. When she got home, she felt carefree and lazy. Half undressed by the bedroom window, she looked over her shoulder through the glass. Sure enough, Mr. Cerroni was working in his garden. He bent down hurriedly at her glance.

Anita laughed and continued to change. She stuffed her clothes in the hamper, glanced at Mr. Cerroni, standing in the middle of his onions, staring straight at her. She snorted and snapped out the light.

The next morning, Anita found a large grocery bag on her doorstep. Radishes, lettuce, onions, carrots, raspberries, young cabbage, and beans. She filled her refrigerator.

Over the next couple of weeks, whenever Anita's vegetable crisper was close to empty, she watched for Mr. Cerroni to appear in his garden. She would leave the curtains open as she changed for bed, and the next morning a brown bag of vegetables would appear on her porch.

One steamy summer day, they were both outside weeding. Anita was nibbling on a young carrot when she felt him watching. She stood up and met his gaze.

"I like the grey one best," he said quietly and then bent back to the rows of tomatoes.

Grey one? My God, he means my grey silk teddy! He's telling me what to wear to bed.

She spit out the carrot and leaving the weeds tossed about the lawn, fled indoors. She downed two glasses of cold water at the sink. That night she closed the curtains tightly before undressing.

After the vegetables were consumed, Anita scrubbed the refrigerator clean. When she ate the last of the packaged Kraft Dinner, she saved some of the cheese powder for the remaining spaghetti noodles. At work, she popped stray grapes into her mouth, retrieving them from the bottom of carts and counters. She developed a talent for palming candies whenever she walked to the washroom.

Salads danced through her dreams, crisp lettuce, crunchy cucumbers, hot radishes. She swore she smelled bacon frying in the mornings. Mr. Cerroni's cherries ripened, bright with invitation.

One evening, when she limped in from a double shift, light-headed with hunger and fatigue, a large brown bag sat on the doorstep. It was filled with a variety of perfect garden delights. As she pulled them from the bag, she pressed each vegetable against her face, inhaling deeply. She danced around the kitchen, clumps of dirt filtering through her fingers. Intoxicating surprises were wrapped in a separate plastic bag—a bottle of Caesar salad dressing and a box of chocolate-covered almonds!

As the salad dressing ran down her chin, Anita wiped it on the back of her arm. It glistened on her skin, stiffening the hairs. She devoured the entire box of candy, melting the chocolate on her tongue, sucking the nuts bare, then crunching each one to bits. Her body shivered with satisfaction. She hadn't felt this full in a long time.

Behind the closed curtains, Anita hesitated. She pinched the blue fabric between her thumb and finger, forming a peephole. Mr. Cerroni's ripening corn swayed in the golden sunshine. He was sitting in a lawn chair, glass in hand, bottle of red wine beside him. He was alone. He seemed smaller than she remembered. Her full stomach gurgled. She took a deep breath and ripped open the curtains. A curious half-smile transformed her face as she smoothed out the grey teddy.

THE END

Proactive

I know this is Hell, but really. There isn't enough room to swing a whip or drive a pitchfork. I'm sick of the agonizing screams, the stench, and the press of humanity. If He would only lighten up. Surely all these people couldn't be that bad? I couldn't squeeze an Irishman in we're so crowded.

He hung up a 'No Vacancy sign', neon red, and headed for New York. The streets were almost as crowded as Hell so it was a good place to start. There was only one way to slow down the population explosion. He needed to get proactive.

First he started with genetic time bombs. Those children growing up in violent homes with inherited makeup similar to their parents were snuffed before adolescence. Nurture or nature, didn't matter when they had both. A slip off a sidewalk into oncoming traffic, a fishbone in the throat, or a fall in the tub sufficed.

He patrolled the streets, striking down anyone decent who had recently fallen in with the wrong crowd. Why wait for them to turn. A quick ticket to Heavenly chorus would prevent any possible fall in grace. Leukemia, kidney failure, or spinal meningitis were the bullets of choice.

Adults toying with thoughts of embezzlement, adultery, or sexual depravity had sudden coronaries. Really, there was only so much temptation these weak humans could handle. Researchers went crazy trying to figure out the unidentified causes of the soaring death rate.

Whenever someone created a movie, song, book, or image that promoted violence or deviant behaviour, they, along with their work, went up in flames in a mysterious fire. Before release, of course.

Eventually, his species cleansing worked. Humans lived harmonious, peaceful lives. Their good habits had the added benefit of longer, more thoughtful lives. Parenting was considered a huge responsibility so fewer children were conceived. At the end of these gentle existences, their pure white souls followed the brilliant light toward Heaven. "Going up" became standard. The opposite path fell into disuse, forgotten. Hell became a vague old myth.

Relieved, he bought a small condo in Florida. Hell could manage without him. *Let the tormented souls punish each other,* he thought.

He loved walking the beach in the morning before the joggers and dog walkers arrived. He loved strolling through the malls at 3:00 pm when most people left to prepare their evening meals. He loved midnight walks in the park when the hard-working populace slept. Existence hadn't been this good in centuries.

The only thing he found annoying was the signs on the side of the bus. "Come to the Universal Church and offer thanks to He who has given us peace."

THE END

About the Author

Learn more about Bonnie online at
http://my.tbaytel.net/bonnieheather/index.htm or checkout her
author page on Amazon or Goodreads. Follow her (Bonnie
Ferrante - Author) on Facebook, on Twitter (Bonnie Ferrante) or
Pinterest.

Please consider leaving a positive review on Amazon or
Goodreads.

Sweet William – first published in *The Wolf's Eye* anthology

Aberrations – a winning entry in the NOWW Fiction contest

Inhale and God Approaches – a winning entry in the *NOWW Magazine* postcard contest

Window Dressing – first published in *The Wolf's Eye* anthology

www.ingramcontent.com/pod-product-compliance
Lightning Source LLC
Chambersburg PA
CBHW070649130626
46555CB00006B/2783